For Enzo

A.S.

© 皮皮與波西：下雪天

繪　　　圖	阿克賽爾・薛弗勒
譯　　　者	酪梨壽司
責任編輯	倪若喬
發 行 人	劉振強
發 行 所	三民書局股份有限公司
	地址　臺北市復興北路386號
	電話　(02)25006600
	郵撥帳號　0009998-5
門 市 部	(復北店) 臺北市復興北路386號
	(重南店) 臺北市重慶南路一段61號
出版日期	初版四刷　2019年6月
編　　　號	S 858151

行政院新聞局登記證局版臺業字第○二○○號

有著作權‧不准侵害

ISBN　978-957-14-6104-5　（精裝）

http://www.sanmin.com.tw　三民網路書店

※本書如有缺頁、破損或裝訂錯誤，請寄回本公司更換。

皮皮與波西

下雪天

阿克賽爾·薛弗勒／圖　　酪梨壽司／譯

三民書局

下ㄒㄧㄚ大ㄉㄚˋ雪ㄒㄩㄝˇ了ㄌㄜ˙！
皮ㄆㄧˊ皮ㄆㄧˊ和ㄏㄢˊ波ㄆㄛ西ㄒㄧ想ㄒㄧㄤˇ出ㄔㄨ門ㄇㄣˊ玩ㄨㄢˊ。

他（ㄊㄚ）們（ㄇㄣ）穿（ㄔㄨㄢ）上（ㄕㄤ）
溫（ㄨㄣ）暖（ㄋㄨㄢˇ）的（ㄉㄜ）毛（ㄇㄠ）衣（ㄧ）一……

條（ㄊㄧㄠˊ）紋（ㄨㄣˊ）的（ㄉㄜ）襪（ㄨㄚˋ）子（ㄗ）……

蓬（ㄆㄥˊ）蓬（ㄆㄥˊ）的（ㄉㄜ）外（ㄨㄞˋ）套（ㄊㄠˋ）……

……防水的靴子，
再戴上舒服的
圍巾和羊毛手套。

然後他們就出門玩雪了。

一路上，他們留下大大的腳印。

他們用舌頭接住從天而降的雪花。

他們甚至變出有雙大翅膀的雪天使。
真是太好玩了。

接著，他們把雪橇拉到小山丘上……

然後從另一邊飛快的衝下來。大喊：

「唷呼！」

接著波西想到一個好點子。
她說：「我們來堆一隻雪鼠吧！」

「但我想要一隻雪兔！」皮皮說。

「雪鼠啦！」波西說。

「雪兔啦！」皮皮說。

波ㄅㄛ西ㄒㄧ好ㄏㄠˇ生ㄕㄥ氣ㄑㄧˋ，
氣ㄑㄧˋ得ㄉㄜ˙抓ㄓㄨㄚ起ㄑㄧˇ雪ㄒㄩㄝˇ鼠ㄕㄨˇ的ㄉㄜ˙頭ㄊㄡˊ丟ㄉㄧㄡ向ㄒㄧㄤˋ皮ㄆㄧˊ皮ㄆㄧˊ。

喔ʊ，天ㄊㄧㄢ啊ㄚ！

皮皮也好生氣，用力推了波西一把，
害她跌在雪地裡。

喔ㄜ，天ㄊㄧㄢ啊ㄚ！

皮皮和波西都覺得好冷好傷心。

可憐的皮皮！可憐的波西！

接著波西做了一件很貼心的事。

她說：「皮皮，對不起，
把你弄得全身都是雪。」

皮皮說：「對不起，我推了妳。」

他們決定一起回到舒服又溫暖的屋內。

他_{ㄊㄚ}們_{ㄇㄣ}脫_{ㄊㄨㄛ}下_{ㄒㄧㄚ}一_ㄧ身_{ㄕㄣ}濕_ㄕ答_{ㄉㄚ}答_{ㄉㄚ}的_{ㄉㄜ}衣_ㄧ物_ㄨ。

然後拿出黏土，捏了老鼠與兔子。

還[ㄏㄞ ˊ]有[ㄧㄡ ˇ]青[ㄑㄧㄥ]蛙[ㄨㄚ]、小[ㄒㄧㄠ ˇ]豬[ㄓㄨ]、小[ㄒㄧㄠ ˇ]鳥[ㄋㄧㄠ ˇ]、大[ㄉㄚ ˋ]象[ㄒㄧㄤ]、乳[ㄖㄨ ˇ]牛[ㄋㄧㄡ ˊ]和[ㄏㄢ ˋ]長[ㄔㄤ ˊ]頸[ㄐㄧㄥ ˇ]鹿[ㄌㄨ ˋ]！

太ㄊㄞˋ棒ㄅㄤˋ啦˙ㄌㄚ！

It was a very snowy day. Pip and Posy wanted to go out and play.

So they put on their woolly jumpers . . .

their puffy coats . . .

their stripy socks . . .

. . . and their waterproof boots, their cosy scarves and their woollen mittens.

Then they went out
into the snow.

Wherever they walked,
they left big footprints.

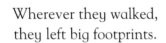

They caught snowflakes on
their tongues.

They even made snow angels
with big wings. It was such good fun.

Next, they pulled their sledge up to the top of the hill . . .

. . . and zoomed down the other side.

"WHEEE!" they shouted.

Then Posy had an idea. "Let's build a snowmouse!" she said.

"But I want a snowrabbit!" said Pip.

"Snowmouse," said Posy.

"SnowRABBIT," said Pip.

Posy was so cross with Pip that she threw
the snowmouse's head at him.

Oh dear!

Then Pip was so cross with Posy
that he pushed her very hard
and she fell into the snow.

Oh dear!

Now Pip and Posy
were **very** cold
and **very** sad indeed.

Poor Pip! Poor Posy!

Then Posy did a very kind thing.

"I am sorry for making you
all snowy, Pip," she said.

"And I am sorry for pushing you,"
said Pip.

They decided to go inside again,
where it was nice and warm.

And then they got out their playdough
and made mice AND rabbits.

They took off all their wet things.

And frogs and pigs and birds, and
elephants and cows and giraffes, as well!

Hooray!

繪者簡介

阿克賽爾·薛弗勒　Axel Scheffler

1957年出生於德國漢堡市，25歲時前往英國就讀巴斯藝術學院。他的插畫風格幽默又不失優雅，最著名的當屬《古飛樂》(Gruffalo) 系列作品，不僅榮獲英國多項繪本大獎，譯作超過40種語言，還曾改編為動畫，深受全球觀眾喜愛，是世界知名的繪本作家。薛弗勒現居英國，持續創作中。

酪梨壽司

畢業於新聞系，擔任媒體記者數年後，前往紐約攻讀企管碩士，回臺後曾任職外商公司行銷部門。婚後旅居日本東京，目前是全職媽媽兼自由撰稿人，出沒於臉書專頁「酪梨壽司」與個人部落格「酪梨壽司的日記」。